MY DOG CAN FLY!

MY DOG CAN FLY!

LEIGH TRESEDER

ILLUSTRATED BY KIM GAMBLE

AN
APPLE
PAPERBACK

SCHOLASTIC INC.
New York Toronto London Auckland Sydney

ISBN 0-590-22504-9

First published in 1993 by Ashton Scholastic Pty Limited.

Copyright © 1993 by Leigh Treseder.
Cover illustrations copyright © 1993 by Ashton Scholastic Pty Limited.
All rights reserved. Published by Scholastic Inc., 555 Broadway, New York, NY, 10012 by arrangement with Ashton Scholastic Pty Limited.

12 11 10 9 8 7 6 5 4 3 2 1   5 6 7 8 9/9 0/0

Printed in U.S.A.   40

First Scholastic printing, April 1995

*For Mom, who encouraged
me to pursue a dream
and whose wisdom and love I miss.*

1

Buster Thompson was ten years old and afraid of the dark. He sat alone in the corner of a railway carriage traveling southwest, to Coolabah. He had one black eye and a heavily bandaged hand.

Night was approaching. He could feel Henry, his pet roly-poly settling down into the corner of his coat pocket. Henry slept there every night.

Buster scuffed his shoes against the seat opposite him. He had never met Great-aunt Tilly. She was probably a witch, anyway, with long strands of greasy gray hair and a large wart on the end of a hooked nose.

"Why do you have to go away?" Buster had complained to his dad. "I don't want to stay with Aunt Tilly."

His father hadn't taken any notice.

"Why can't I stay home on my own?"

"Don't be ridiculous!" his father snapped. "You're only a child."

So here he was — staring out of the window. The countryside whizzed past. What on earth would he do on a farm? He hadn't bothered to ask if he could bring his surfboard. Coolabah was miles from the beach.

"Dad should have let me bring my skateboard," Buster muttered. "I bet it'll be boring."

His father had said there were plenty of interesting things for a boy to do in the country. Buster was not convinced. The train rattled on. Would they ever arrive? He might be stuck onboard the train forever.

He watched the sun disappear behind the line of distant hills. It would be dark soon. A woman sitting on the other side of the car smiled at him. He pretended not to notice. You can't fool me with a smile, he thought. He knew not to talk to strangers.

Crash!

The door that separated the next car banged open and the conductor appeared. Mr. Thompson had left Buster in the conductor's care.

"Next stop is yours, sonny," he said. "About two more minutes."

At last! Buster jumped up and grabbed his black sports bag from under the seat while the conductor collected Buster's suitcase from the overhead rack. Henry! He checked his coat pocket. Yes! His friend was still there.

The train slowed. Buster followed the conductor. The end of the platform flashed past the window and the train clattered and banged to a stop. They stepped out of the car. Buster glanced around anxiously. The station lights glared down at him.

The platform was empty.

But wait! Who was that?

A woman emerged from the waiting room. Could this be Great-aunt Tilly? Sturdy legs laced into sensible shoes marched toward them.

"Buster Thompson!" she cried. "You haven't changed a bit since you were a toddler! I'm your Great-aunt Tilly. I've been looking forward to seeing you again."

I don't remember you, Buster thought. He didn't reply.

The conductor was obviously relieved to see her. After a quick conversation, he blew his whistle and returned to the train. It pulled out, leaving Buster behind.

Buster was wary. He eyed the woman. Well, she didn't have a hooked nose. Or a wart. But she did have gray hair. She talked nonstop as she struggled to carry the suitcase out into the parking area. Buster remained silent.

"You seem to have been in the wars," she remarked, and glanced at his black eye and bandaged hand. "A few days in the fresh country air and you'll be as good as new."

They stopped beside a battered truck. Buster

was amazed! Old ladies don't drive trucks, he thought.

But this one obviously did. She shoved his case onto the back of the truck then opened the passenger door. "Hop in. We'll be home soon. I've made a big pot of vegetable soup for tea. Ned's keeping an eye on it."

Buster shuddered. He hated soup. And who was Ned?

Aunt Tilly crunched the gears. The truck lurched forward. Buster was flung back into his seat. They kangarooed in leaps and bounds out into the night. It was completely dark now.

The headlights probed the road ahead. Buster stared out of the window. He couldn't see a thing. There were no streetlights out here.

The road wound on. Aunt Tilly crunched the gears constantly. Gosh, thought Buster, she'll strip the gears. But Aunt Tilly didn't seem to think there was anything wrong with the way she drove. She just kept on talking, all about when Buster was a baby — how she remembered his blond hair and big brown eyes, etcetera, etcetera.

Buster was drowsy. It had been a long day. He leaned his head against the window. His face ached.

He remembered the fight with Big Tim Heggarty in the school yard. He'd landed a couple of good punches before a teacher intervened. They'd

4

been making Mother's Day presents and Heggarty had taunted him. He'd said that Buster's mother hadn't really died. She'd just walked out and left because she didn't like Buster.

Well, Buster had given him something to think about. Two things in fact! Two beautiful, big, black eyes. He touched his bandaged hand. It was worth it!

Aunt Tilly glanced across. "Nearly home now, Buster."

It's not my home, he thought, looking out of the window.

The headlights swung off the main road. The truck bumped down a narrow track, swerved violently, then bounced. Buster's head almost hit the roof.

"Sorry about the potholes," Aunt Tilly laughed.

They clattered over a wooden bridge and stopped in front of a gate. Aunt Tilly clambered out, opened it, then drove the truck through.

Suddenly, shadows loomed like huge monsters in front of the headlights! They jumped up all around the truck. Buster saw flashing teeth and tails flying wildly.

The truck jerked to a stop.

What was that? Buster could have sworn he saw something flying straight at them. Aunt Tilly flicked the headlight switch and the lights snapped off.

"Down, dogs. Down!" she shouted.

Buster looked around him. He must have imagined it. Well, he wasn't getting out with all those dogs barking at him. There must be hundreds!

Lights were switched on and lit up the farmhouse.

A man appeared in the doorway.

"Would you get the bags, Ned?" called Aunt Tilly. "And shut the gate, please."

She came around to the passenger door. "Buster's exhausted. I'll give him a quick tea and put him to bed."

Buster wasn't used to having someone organize him like this. But he was too tired to argue.

"The dogs don't bite," she reassured and pushed them out of the way.

Buster hesitated, then jumped down. He followed her across the yard, watching the dogs nervously. As they went into the house, Aunt Tilly said, "Chopper's the only dog allowed inside. He's special." She smiled. "Sit down. I'll get your soup."

In no time at all, Buster found himself climbing into a huge old-fashioned bed.

"I'll leave the hallway light on all night," Aunt Tilly said. "It can be a bit scary if you wake up in a strange house."

Buster was relieved. Now he wouldn't have to tell Aunt Tilly he was afraid of the dark. He thought about Henry. He must remember to take him out of his coat pocket in the morning.

As he drifted off to sleep, he thought back over the day. Aunt Tilly didn't seem too bad. Maybe she wasn't a witch. Ned seemed a bit strange, though. He'd have to find out about him tomorrow.

2

Buster hated pudding. Dad made it often and it was revolting. You had to strain the lumps through your teeth! Other people bought smooth, lump-free pudding in cartons from the supermarket. Not Dad. He insisted on making his own. He said it was an old family recipe and he always made Buster eat every last drop.

Buster stared at the bowl in front of him. He wished it would disappear. It was his second night with Aunt Tilly and for tea she had served Jell-O and pudding for dessert. The Jell-O had been wonderful. He had demolished the quivering green mound after carefully scraping the pudding off. Moodily, he pushed his spoon around the remaining yellow puddle.

Perhaps Chopper would eat it. The black-and-white border collie under the table pushed against Buster's knees. Aunt Tilly had gone to lock up the chickens for the night and Ned was feeding the other dogs in the yard. Buster had been left at the table to finish his dessert.

He looked through the open kitchen door. No one was coming. He placed the bowl on the floor. "Chopper. Here, boy. Have some pudding."

The dog came out from under the table, wagging his tail. He sniffed at the bowl and began licking the pudding with loud slurps. Buster stared, amazed. Chopper actually seemed to like it!

Suddenly, something incredible happened. Chopper let out a bloodcurdling howl, his eyes turned red, glowed brightly like traffic lights and his tail started to spin around.

Before Buster could say anything, Chopper rose into the air like a helicopter, hovered near the ceiling then — wham! — shot out through the door. Buster flung the bowl onto the table and ran after him. The dog was circling above the farmhouse, teeth bared in what seemed like a grin.

"Dogs don't fly!"

Footsteps crunched on the gravel behind him. He spun around. It was Ned coming through the gate. Ned, he'd discovered, was Aunt Tilly's brother. But unlike Aunt Tilly, Ned was a man of few words.

Buster glanced up at the sky. Chopper was nowhere to be seen. Had Ned noticed anything strange? He seemed to have a twinkle in his eye,

but didn't say anything as he continued on, into the house.

Did I imagine it? Buster wondered. He followed Ned indoors. "I didn't eat that pudding," Buster muttered to himself.

"Pardon?" said Aunt Tilly as she walked in behind him.

"Nothing."

Buster was thoroughly confused.

Aunt Tilly cleared the table. "After I've washed up, I'll have a look at your sore hand," she said, stacking dishes in the sink. "I have a wonderful ointment that works like magic. It will cure anything."

Buster panicked. He knew she was a witch! She must have put a spell on Chopper. *Now she's going to put a spell on me!* "My hand doesn't need any ointment," he shouted. "It's better!"

He raced out of the kitchen and up the stairs to the room where he'd slept last night. "I'm getting out of here!"

He grabbed his coat, ran downstairs, past an astonished Aunt Tilly and out through the door.

"What's wrong with Buster?" Aunt Tilly called to Ned. "Go and see where he's gone, will you?"

Ned found Buster in the woodshed. He was scrabbling around on the dusty ground. "What are you looking for, son?" asked Ned quietly.

"I'm trying to find Henry. And when I do, I'm leaving this place," Buster shouted.

11

"Who's Henry?"

"He's my pet roly-poly. I brought him with me from home. In my coat pocket. I put him out here this morning. It looked like a good place to keep him. Now I'm taking him back."

Ned didn't reply. He leaned against the wall.

"Well, don't just stand there, watching," Buster yelled angrily, "help me find him!"

"It might be better to wait 'til morning," Ned offered. "It's getting too dark now."

Buster was defiant. He kept searching among the woodpile.

"Maybe Henry found a lady friend and they've gone off together somewhere," Ned suggested.

"Henry wouldn't leave me!" Great gulping sobs started to shake Buster's body.

Ned waited patiently until the sobs died down. "It's too dark to search for Henry now and you can't find your way home at night. Maybe we'd better go back inside. We can look for Henry in the morning."

Buster stood there as Ned walked across the yard to the house, then followed reluctantly. Ned didn't say anything further. He flashed Aunt Tilly a warning glance as he went through the kitchen to the living room.

"Well," Aunt Tilly said in a bright voice, "why don't you go and have your bath now, before Ned wants the bathroom. He likes to have a long soak."

As Buster went upstairs he heard Aunt Tilly say, "That child needs a mother."

He muttered to himself, "I'm going to find Henry tomorrow and get away from here. They can't make me stay."

The next morning he searched the woodpile again. Chopper bounded over to him. The dog certainly looked normal. Where had he been the night before? Ned wandered in and asked Buster if he'd like a ride on the motorbike. He was going to move some sheep. Buster hesitated. What about Henry?

"I'm sure Henry's all right," Ned said, as if reading his mind. "Chopper would love some company."

The dog barked. He jumped up, tail wagging, and put his front paws on Buster's chest. He rubbed Chopper's ears. It looked like he had found a new friend. Maybe Henry had found a lady roly-poly to go off with. Anyway, a roly-poly was probably happier in a woodpile.

Buster decided to hop on the bike behind Ned. Chopper jumped up, squeezed in between them, and off they roared.

It turned out to be great fun rounding up sheep. Buster spent the whole day with Ned and Chopper. He went to bed that night, exhausted, and fell asleep instantly.

*   *   *

Some hours later, Buster became aware of something damp touching his hand. He woke with a start. His heart pounded. A shadow was beside his bed. His mouth was too dry to scream. The back of his neck prickled, as if a spider was walking on him.

What was it?

The shadow moved. A slant of light spilled into the bedroom from the hallway and reflected on a patch of white. It was Chopper! Buster breathed a sigh of relief. The dog padded over to the door and whined.

"What is it?" whispered Buster. "What do you want me to do?" Chopper whined again.

Buster clambered out of bed and reached for his coat. The night air was cold. He pulled on a pair of jeans over his pajamas and stuffed his feet into his shoes. Chopper padded silently down the stairs.

"Wait for me." Buster crept after him.

The dog went into the kitchen and pawed at the fridge door.

Buster opened the refrigerator. A bowl of pudding shimmered on the top shelf.

He looked at Chopper. The dog seemed to be laughing. His tongue lolled out from the side of his mouth and his head shook.

He checked the pudding again. It was still shimmering!

3

Chopper barked.

"Quiet boy," whispered Buster. "You'll wake everyone up."

He hesitated, then pulled the bowl of pudding out of the fridge. It looked just like the huge yellow moon in the night sky.

"If this pudding works like the last time, I'm going for a ride with you, Chopper."

He placed the bowl on the floor. The dog slurped greedily at it. Yellow specks flicked onto his face and clung to his whiskers. Buster held his breath.

It happened. Exactly like last time! Chopper let out a bloodcurdling howl, his eyes turned red like traffic lights, and his tail started to spin around. Buster raced to the door. Had Ned or Aunt Tilly been woken by the noise? He looked up the stairs. No one appeared. The rest of the house was quiet. As he turned back, he was just in time to see Chopper lift off like a helicopter, then lower himself down again.

Of course! That's how the dog got his name! But would he still be able to fly with Buster on his back? There was only one way to find out.

Buster took a flying leap toward Chopper. He just managed to scramble on his back before the dog rose up and hovered over the sink. Buster clung on tight to the dog's collar with his unbandaged hand. Chopper zoomed out through the open window.

It worked! They circled once above the farmhouse, then flew off, into the night.

In all the excitement, Buster completely forgot that he was afraid of the dark. "Where are we going?" he shouted.

Chopper didn't reply. He might be able to fly, but he couldn't talk. He just turned his head to the left, bared his teeth in a grin, and continued on.

Chopper's bright-red eyes lit up the sky directly ahead of them. But when Buster looked down toward the ground, he couldn't see a thing. Where were they?

A bright light appeared in the distance.

"Chopper, what's that?" Buster cried out in alarm.

More lights. Maybe they were spaceships. What if he was spirited away to another planet? Or what if it was the air force sending fighter planes to intercept an unidentified flying object? The two of them, boy and dog, might be blasted out of the sky by a missile.

The lights came closer and closer. Buster was frightened. He felt like this sometimes when he was in the surf and about to be dumped by a huge wave.

Still more lights appeared. Some were colored, others winked. Gasping with relief, Buster realized they were approaching town. It must be Coolabah. Chopper tilted his nose toward the ground. Now Buster could see the outlines of houses and shops.

Without warning, a brilliant white light appeared and raced toward them with a deafening roar. Buster closed his eyes in panic. "This is it! I'm dead!"

He nearly fell off the dog in fright as a long mournful whistle sounded underneath them. Buster opened his eyes just in time to see a freight train disappearing into the distance! "We must have been following the railway line." He laughed, weak with relief.

Chopper flew lower and lower. The shops became clearer as they cruised down the main street.

Crash!

The sound of breaking glass shattered the night. Buster spotted a man wearing a cap, outside what appeared to be a jewelry shop. He had smashed the glass door and his hand was through the hole, trying to undo the lock.

"What are we going to do?" Buster shouted into Chopper's ear, as the dog gained height and swerved away.

The man was now in the shop. He hadn't noticed them. Just as well! A cold sweat trickled down Buster's back. He hadn't planned on meeting any robbers tonight!

What would Chopper do?

He soon found out. The dog flew down and circled a small brick building. The sign out front said, POLICE.

Chopper looked over his shoulder as if to say, "Do something!"

Buster became angry. What did the dog expect him to do? They couldn't land in the yard. Imagine what the police would say if Buster rushed into the station and told them about the break-in.

"What are you doing out by yourself so late at night?" they'd ask.

He could hardly tell them he'd just flown in on a dog! But what should he do? There had to be a way of alerting the police. Buster thought hard. Then he remembered he had a used chocolate-bar wrapper in his coat pocket. It gave him an idea.

"Slow down a bit," he shouted to Chopper. Buster gripped his knees tightly against the dog, let go of the collar, then fumbled in his pocket to find the torn paper and old pencil stub that he always carried around.

But wait a minute! He wouldn't be able to work with only one hand. He ripped the bandage off the sore one. Working quickly, he made a paper airplane. It wasn't one of his best, but it would have to do. He'd never made one while flying on a dog before!

The inside of the wrapper was white. He made sure that the printing on the outside was folded in and hidden. Now he could write on the plane. He managed to scribble in rough capital letters on one wing, *ROBBER*. On the other wing, he spelled out *JEWELER*. He wasn't sure if jeweler had one L or two, but he spelled it with one.

Chopper circled toward the front of the building. Buster took aim and threw the paper airplane as hard as he could. In through the open door it sped.

What a shot! It landed right on the desk in front of a startled policeman. His papers scattered everywhere.

"What was that?" Buster heard the policeman shout.

Two officers ran out through the front door. One was a woman. "I don't know where the plane came from. Something's going on. We'd better check," she said.

The other officer glanced up. "Wait a minute. What's that? Over there near the trees?"

Chopper increased speed. The dog gained height rapidly and they disappeared from sight.

Now what?

"Oh, no!" groaned Buster. "Not the shops again. Please, Chopper. Let's just go home."

But Chopper didn't listen. He roared back up the main street to look for the robber. And there he was! Coming out of the jewelry shop with a bag clutched tightly under one arm. Buster looked back. The police car turned onto the main street, its blue light flashing. The siren wailed and the car sped forward. They'd seen the robber. The man ran, veered across the road and into the park. Chopper was close behind. He drew alongside. Buster stuck out his foot and tripped the robber!

CRASH! BANG!

The robber fell heavily. The bag dropped from his grip and he cursed loudly. Buster glanced back and saw that the police car had pulled up at the edge of the park. Its headlights blazed across the grass. The officers ran over to the fallen man.

"Quick, Chopper. Get out of here!"

The dog zoomed up over the top of some very tall trees. Buster's stomach lurched. They swerved around in a U-turn, toward the blue flashing light and saw three people headed toward the police car. The robber had been caught.

Chopper skimmed over more trees and away from the park. Buster laughed and laughed. What

a joke! He could just imagine the robber saying to the police, "An alien was chasing me!"

"What did you say?"

"An alien was chasing me. You should have seen it!"

The police would be amazed.

Buster couldn't remember anything as funny as this in ages. Chopper flew on. Buster felt tired now and hoped they were heading for home. He didn't want any more excitement tonight. It seemed like hours since they'd left the farm. He grew sleepier and held on tight, afraid that he might fall off the dog. Would they ever get back? What if Chopper ran out of fuel? Surely it hadn't been this far?

Just when Buster was certain that they were hopelessly lost, Chopper dropped down, down, down — toward a single light below them. At last! It was the farm. Chopper appeared to be getting weaker. They bumped to the ground outside the kitchen window. Buster got off, stiff and weary. The dog was exhausted, too, and crouched in the dirt, panting.

Buster clambered onto the windowsill and called, "Here, boy. Jump up."

But the dog just stared at him without moving. Buster hesitated, then jumped down and gathered the dog up clumsily into his arms. He really had to struggle, but eventually managed to push

Chopper through the window onto the kitchen sink.

Buster clambered through the window, picked up the dog again and tiptoed up the stairs to his bedroom. It was almost morning. Just as well he didn't have to go to school today.

He dumped the dog down on top of the bed, then, too tired to even take off his coat, he climbed in, too. Chopper sighed gratefully. The dog rested its head on its paws. Buster rolled onto his side and wrapped one arm around the dog, feeling its warmth.

As he drifted off to sleep, Buster remembered how his mom used to leave the hallway light on for him at night. She'd laughed gently at his suggestion that a robber might creep down the hall in the dark, but she'd always left the light on, anyway. After she died, he couldn't understand why his dad insisted that it be turned off each night.

"You're too old to have the light on, Buster," he'd said.

Thank goodness Aunt Tilly left *her* hall light on. He didn't want to meet anymore robbers tonight.

4

It was Sunday afternoon.

"I'm not going to a dumb old country school," yelled Buster. "I came here for a vacation."

"You *are* going and that's enough of your nonsense," Aunt Tilly replied in a firm voice.

Aunt Tilly had dropped a bombshell when she told Buster he was to be enrolled at the local school the next day.

"Dad didn't tell me I'd have to go to school. He's only gone for a few weeks. I can catch up on my lessons when I get home."

She ignored Buster and continued, "Ned can take you tomorrow in the truck. After that you'll be able to catch the school bus. It stops just down the road."

Buster was mad. He charged out of the kitchen, slamming the door. "I won't go! She can't make me. I won't know anybody."

He stormed down to the woodshed. It had become his own private hideaway. A place to be by himself when he wanted to think.

The shed was very old. It was made from corrugated iron and had only three walls. The front was open to the weather and everything was covered in dust and wood chips, but the roof was still intact. Buster had found lots of interesting bits and pieces on the wooden bench that ran across the back wall. Rusty nails, old horseshoes, tools, and an ancient tin hat (probably left over from a war). Even a skeleton! Well, only a cow's head, but it was still pretty exciting.

Buster perched on top of a pile of logs and stared moodily out across the paddocks. Two kookaburras flew into a gum tree next to the shed. They peered down at him, heads cocked to one side. Buster felt uncomfortable.

Kookaburras were meat-eaters. What if they thought he was a giant lizard and flew down and bit a chunk out of him? Their beady eyes stared at him without blinking. What were they thinking? One started to laugh. Just a gurgle at first. Then the second bird joined in. Their high-pitched laughter became louder and louder, almost deafening him.

"Shut up!" he shouted. "Buzz off!"

He hurled a wood chip at the tormenters. The birds flew away, still laughing.

"Rotten birds. It's not fair. Everyone's against me."

He felt miserable. He sat there, chin in his hands and thought about tomorrow. What would the new school be like? He wouldn't have any friends. He supposed the teachers would be horrible.

Then, something hanging up high, at the back of the shed, caught his eye. What was it? Buster clambered across the top of the woodpile and stood on the bench. He stretched upward. It was just out of reach. He needed extra height. A log. Maybe that would do. He dragged one off the pile and positioned it on the bench. Still not high enough.

He looked around the shed and spied an old broom leaning against the wall. Just the thing! He knocked some of the cobwebs off the strange object. Clunk! It hit the bench.

What luck! It was an old leather flying helmet and goggles. He'd seen pictures of pilots in World War II wearing gear like this. It was exactly what he needed.

"I wonder if they belong to Ned? He might let me use them."

Buster ran down to the paddocks. Ned was riding the motorbike. Chopper was crouched on the seat behind him. They'd been moving sheep from the top of the hill to the home paddock. Buster was constantly amazed at the way the dog kept his balance on the bike.

"G'day, Buster," said Ned. "What have you got there?"

"I found these in the woodshed. Are they yours?"

"Yes, they're mine. I'd forgotten all about them."

Dozens of questions crowded into Buster's mind. But before he had a chance to ask Ned any of them, the dinner gong was sounded. Aunt Tilly rang it whenever a meal was ready.

Dinnertime," said Ned. "Hop on the back of the bike. I'll give you a ride to the house."

Buster climbed up behind him and they roared off, with Chopper running alongside.

"Can I borrow the helmet and goggles?" Buster shouted into Ned's ear.

"Sure."

Buster was lucky. Ned didn't ask any questions. As they came to a stop, he saw Aunt Tilly. She was standing in the kitchen doorway, arms folded across a brightly patterned apron. This one was covered in pink and purple roses. She had a number of them. Buster thought they were all revolting, but Aunt Tilly loved them and had worn a different one each day.

"Tea's ready. Wash your hands and I'll serve it up."

Buster hoped there'd be pudding for dessert. He was really keen to try out the helmet and goggles. But no such luck! Aunt Tilly had made apple pie and ice cream.

"Is there any pudding?" he asked.

"Not tonight," she replied. "I made the ice cream as a special treat. Thought it might cheer you up about tomorrow."

Buster's heart sank. In all the excitement of finding the flying gear, he'd completely forgotten about the new school. If only there was some pudding then he'd be able to escape on Chopper. But there'd be no flying tonight.

As he lay in bed later that night, Buster remembered Big Tim Heggarty. He hoped there wouldn't be a bully like him in the new school.

The next morning, Buster went with Ned and Chopper in the truck.

"I've spoken to the principal," Aunt Tilly had said.

"You won't have to wear a uniform, because you'll only be here for a few weeks."

That had been the only good thing about the day. Buster felt really cool wearing his sneakers instead of gross black school shoes.

The principal at his school in the city was really strict about school uniforms. Once, Buster had forged a note from his father. It read BUSTER'S SCHOOL SHOES HAVE A HOLE IN THEM AND I CAN'T

AFFORD TO BUY HIM A NEW PAIR JUST YET. HE'LL
HAVE TO WEAR HIS SNEAKERS, INSTEAD.

But the principal hadn't been fooled. She said
that fathers didn't print. They used handwriting.
So Buster was placed on detention for two weeks!

As they bumped along the road to Coolabah,
Buster stroked Chopper's head. The other dogs
had run around the truck barking, as they'd driven
off from the farm, but Ned had told them all to
stay.

"Why is Chopper the only dog allowed in the
house?" Buster asked Ned.

"He's my friend.

"How did he get his name?"

There was silence for so long that Buster began
to think he wouldn't get an answer. Eventually
the reply came.

"I called him Chopper when he was just a pup,"
Ned said, with a small smile.

He didn't offer any further information.

Buster was dying to know if Ned knew about
Chopper's adventures, but he wasn't quite game
enough to ask. Besides, they had arrived at Coolabah Public School.

It didn't look like a city school. No concrete
playgrounds with hundreds of children shouting
and playing. Just a few small buildings sur-
rounded by grass and trees and a wire fence. Cows
grazed in a nearby paddock.

"You must remember to always close the gate

when you're out in the country," Ned said as they walked through. "Otherwise cows and sheep wander where they're not supposed to be."

School had already started for the day. The thought of walking into a strange classroom with all the kids staring at him made Buster feel sick in the stomach. He wished the floor would open up and swallow him! Ned knocked on a door that said PRINCIPAL, in gold letters.

"Come in," boomed a deep voice.

The door opened and Buster saw a tall man with glasses and a bald head. "You must be Buster," he said. "Sit down, sit down. My name is Mr. Baker. I'm the principal of Coolabah Public School and I hope you'll be very happy while you're here with us."

Fat chance of that, Buster thought.

"I'll just tell you the school rules and then I'll take you along to your classroom," Mr. Baker stated.

That'd be right. Why are there always rules? Buster said to himself. Anybody would think it was the army!

But there didn't seem to be that many and before long the principal was saying to Ned, "I'll take Buster along to his class now, and you can pick him up at three o'clock."

Buster cast a desperate glance at Ned, but he didn't seem to notice. He just said good-bye and walked out.

"Come along, come along," Mr. Baker said. "Don't want to waste the day. You'll just be in time for mathematics."

"Oh, great!" Buster mumbled. "I hate math."

"Beg your pardon?"

"Nothing."

He followed the principal reluctantly.

"Excuse me, Miss Entwhistle. This is your new pupil, Buster Thompson."

Chairs scraped backward. Heads turned and Buster felt dozens of eyes staring at him.

"Good morning, children," boomed the principal.

"Good morning, Mr. Baker," chanted the class.

"Welcome to the class, Buster. Come and sit down front, near me," the teacher said.

Buster's feet were glued to the floor. He stared at his shoes, but they just wouldn't move.

The principal left.

Buster slowly raised his head. He was astonished to see that the teacher was quite young. Her long blond hair was tied in a ponytail with a red ribbon that matched her short red skirt. Wow! They didn't have teachers like this at Fairmont Public School.

She pulled out an empty chair and Buster found himself walking past the staring eyes. He wished he could just disappear! If only the floor would open up. But it didn't, so he sat down in front of the teacher.

The morning passed in a blur.

At lunchtime, a big tough boy with black hair and mean-looking eyes swaggered up. He poked Buster in the chest several times. "So you think you're Mr. Cool from the city in your sneakers, do you? Well, me and my gang run things around here. So you'd better watch out!"

"Oh, leave him alone, McGinty," came a second voice.

A small boy with red hair appeared from around the corner of a building.

"Butt out, Morgan," snarled the bully.

About half a dozen other boys closed around Buster and Morgan in a semicircle.

Here we go again, Buster thought. He eyed the gang to see which one he'd go for first. Just as the situation was starting to look really nasty, Mr. Baker appeared in the distance. The gang quickly melted away behind the building.

"Stay away from McGinty," advised the red-haired boy. "He's really mean. Picks on everyone."

Buster was amazed that someone so small would have the courage to stand up to the over-weight bully.

"Daniel Morgan's my name. My friends call me Danny," he grinned.

"Hi! Thanks for your help," Buster replied, "but I usually fight my own battles."

"Well, don't tangle with that lot," Danny warned. "Come on. I'll show you around."

Buster was introduced to some of the other kids. They were all talking about a robbery in the town on Saturday night.

"Did you hear about the spaceship and the robber?"

"It wasn't a spaceship. It was an alien."

Buster smiled secretly to himself. The kids continued talking.

McGinty appeared again. "I could beat a robber any day."

"Oh, yeah?" scoffed a girl with blond braids.

"I'd give him a karate kick in the throat," McGinty snapped. He was getting angry. "What would you know. You're only a girl!"

"You can't do karate. You're so fat you'd only fall flat on your face," taunted Blond Braids.

The kids shrieked with laughter.

McGinty was furious. Just as he opened his mouth to retort, the bell rang to signal the end of lunchtime. Still laughing, the group broke up and moved toward the classrooms.

"I'll get you for that," shouted the bully to the back of the disappearing crowd.

Buster glanced sideways at the girl as they entered the classroom. He hadn't noticed her during the morning lessons. She didn't appear to be worried by the threat.

Most of the kids seemed friendly. Except for McGinty. Buster would need to stay away from him.

5

Buster dreaded getting onto the school bus each morning. McGinty and his gang always spread themselves across the backseats like tentacles. Wherever Buster sat, they reached out to torment him. He'd even tried sitting behind the driver, but that didn't stop the bullies. They weren't afraid of anyone.

Every day was a new nightmare. They ripped his bus pass off his bag and hurled it out of the window. Aunt Tilly had to get a new one. Dead spiders were thrown at him. He hated spiders. Once, a lizard was stuffed inside the collar of his shirt. It was still alive and wriggled and squirmed all the way down his back. Another day, his schoolbag was grabbed. The gang tossed it from one to the other.

"C'mon, Thompson. Don't you want your lunch today?"

Every time he made a grab for it, the bag was

34

thrown to someone else. Eventually he caught it, but his lunch was squashed.

The daily taunts continued. Buster hated it, but he was determined not to show his fear in front of McGinty. He followed Danny's advice and tried to stay away from the bully.

At lunchtime he started playing cricket with a group that included Erin, the girl with blond braids. The first day he joined in, Buster was horrified to see a girl on the field. He soon realized that girls could play just as well as boys when she clean bowled his middle stump with her first ball!

"Howzat!" she yelled, feet planted wide apart, arms raised, like a miniature version of a blond Merv Hughes.

Buster couldn't believe his eyes. Fancy being bowled out by a girl! The next day was better. The two of them were on the same team and it was Buster's turn to bowl. Michael Carter had been batting since the game began and it was almost time for the bell to go. Buster's team was desperate for a wicket.

Taking a long run up, Buster hurled the ball down toward the stumps. Carter took a mighty swing and cracked the ball high into the air toward the boundary.

"It's a six!" shouted Carter's partner, deciding not to run.

Buster's heart sank. He'd never get a wicket.

Then he watched, amazed. Erin raced across the field toward the speeding ball. She caught it with one outstretched hand, just inside the boundary.

"What a catch!" Danny cried.

"He's out!" screamed another fielder.

Erin charged in toward the pitch. The team crowded around Erin and Buster, thumping them on their backs and jumping up and down with excitement.

"Great catch," Buster offered to Erin.

"Well, it was a pretty good bowl," she replied.

Buster felt proud! Maybe he'd get to play for Australia one day. Coolabah School wasn't too bad after all. Except for McGinty and his band of bullies. It was a pity none of the cricket kids caught his bus. They all seemed to live on the other side of town.

The following day, Buster found himself in trouble again. As usual, in the morning, when the bus arrived at school he was one of the first off and through the school gate. He wanted to avoid McGinty, who was always one of the last.

During the morning lessons, the class was startled when Miss Entwhistle let out a shriek and ran from the room.

"Shoo, shoo! You stupid cows. Get out of here!"

The children rushed to the windows. Four cows were casually munching on the teacher's prize flowers. Miss Entwhistle slapped the cows on their rumps, trying to drive them out through the

36

open gate. After a couple of minutes, she suc-
ceeded and came storming back to the classroom.
The children scrambled into their seats.

"Who left the gate open?" she demanded,
flushed and angry.

Nobody answered.

"Well, somebody must have done it!"

McGinty put up his hand. "Please, Miss. It was
the new city kid. But he probably didn't know any
better." The bully smirked.

Buster was stunned.

What a lie! McGinty was really out to get him.
And he was clever enough to make it seem as
though he was sticking up for Buster.

"Stand up, Buster Thompson," the teacher said
sternly. "Did you leave the gate open?"

"No, I did not!" he retorted.

"I realize you may not understand how impor-
tant it is to close gates when you are out in the
country," said the teacher, "but if you lie to me,
you'll be in much worse trouble."

"I didn't leave the gate open," Buster repeated.

Miss Entwhistle stared at him. He stared back,
defiantly.

"Well it had better not happen again. I've put
a lot of time and effort into that garden. I was
going to enter it in the annual competition. Now
it's ruined."

She looked as though she might burst into tears.
"You can help me tidy up the mess at lunchtime."

37

Buster was furious! He sat down. No cricket today, thanks to McGinty. Buster fumed for the rest of the lesson. But even though he was angry, he did feel sorry for the teacher. The plants had been looking very colorful. Now they were just a trampled mass.

As they left the classroom, Buster rushed up to McGinty.

"You dirty, rotten liar! You know I didn't leave the gate open. I bet you did it. Just to get me into trouble."

"You can't prove anything," sneered McGinty.

Buster let fly with a punch that landed squarely on McGinty's nose. Surprised, the bully stood still for a moment then wiped the back of his hand slowly across his face. He looked shocked at the sight of bright-red blood smeared across his fingers.

"Why you little — "

Buster fell to the ground with the force of the return punch.

"Fight! Fight! Fight!" chanted dozens of voices.

Children rushed from everywhere. The two boys rolled over and over on the dusty ground.

Suddenly there was silence. The principal had arrived, but the two fighters didn't realize it until they were each grabbed by the neck and hauled to their feet.

"Enough! I will not have fighting in this school.

You know the rules. Come to my office immediately."

Buster felt miserable. His face hurt and so did his hand. Oh, no! The pocket of his shirt was half torn off. Aunt Tilly would be mad at him. He trailed behind Mr. Baker into his office. McGinty followed, holding a dirty handkerchief to his bloody nose.

"Now, what's this all about?" demanded the principal, closing the door behind the boys.

Neither spoke.

"Buster? Sean?"

Still no answer. Buster stared straight ahead. McGinty was fidgeting beside him.

Mr. Baker raved on for several minutes about how he wouldn't tolerate fighting in his school, and then asked again what the fight was about. There was no reply.

"Well, you leave me no choice. You will both be punished. You can each write out two hundred lines — I must not fight at school. I want them on my desk by nine o'clock tomorrow. Dismissed!"

Rage boiled up inside Buster. First, Miss Entwhistle had ruined his lunchtime cricket, and now Mr. Baker was punishing him. As they left the office together, Buster hissed to McGinty, "I'll get you for this!"

* * *

Buster lay in bed rubbing his wrist and flexing his fingers. His hand ached. No wonder, after writing two hundred lines.

Aunt Tilly had been cross with him for getting into a fight. He had to get even with McGinty. There must be a way.

Gradually, an idea took shape in his mind. He lay there for a few minutes, sorting out the details, then jumped out of bed and searched the bottom of the cupboard until he found the helmet and goggles.

With his flashlight stuffed into his backpack he crept to the bedroom door. Were Aunt Tilly and Ned still up? He listened — not a sound. He tiptoed down the stairs. Chopper appeared from nowhere like a silent ghost and followed close behind.

There had been pudding for tea!

Buster reached the kitchen, quietly closed the door behind him and turned on the light. He wasn't afraid of the dark when he was with Chopper, but he needed to be able to see clearly.

Buster pulled the leather helmet over his head and down over both ears. He admired his reflection in the window. Just like a movie star!

Now it was Chopper's turn. Stretching the strap on the goggles, Buster carefully fitted them over the dog's head. He adjusted the front so that Chopper could see.

They were ready for action!

Buster took the bowl of pudding from the fridge and set it on the floor. Chopper greedily slurped it down.

It was happening again! The dog let out a blood-curdling howl, his eyes turned red, and his tail started to spin around. Buster jumped on his back and hung onto Chopper's collar. They zoomed out through the window and into the night.

"To the school!" cried Buster.

As they flew through the dark, Buster thought about McGinty. Boy, was he going to get a shock!

Soon the lights of the town appeared. In no time at all, they were landing in the school yard. There was no doubt about Chopper. He certainly knew his way around! Buster climbed off the dog. It was pitch-black. He reached into his backpack for the flashlight.

Holding onto Chopper's collar with one hand and the flashlight with the other, Buster moved forward slowly. He headed toward the garden shed behind the school buildings.

During the week, painters had arrived to completely repaint the school. The paint was locked in the shed, but the tins used for cleaning brushes were stored behind the shed. Mr. Baker had given the children a strict warning. The painter's preparation area was out of bounds.

Buster was almost at the shed, when he heard

a noise. He froze, heart pounding. There it was again! Somebody else was nearby. Who could it be? He switched off the flashlight.

Then he heard a chewing sound. Whoever it was obviously didn't eat with their mouth shut. The noise continued. Chopper hadn't barked, so it must be someone friendly. Buster decided to be brave and investigate. He tightened his grip on the dog's collar and crept forward. It was hard to see without the flashlight. He pushed one foot out along the ground, then the other, feeling his way as if by radar.

Plop! Plop! Splat!

What a disgusting smell! Buster wrinkled his nose and snapped on the flashlight. Two big brown eyes stared at him from over a fence and a mouth chewed slowly, around and around.

Buster laughed out loud. It was only a cow! In the cold night air, steam rose from the fresh pile of cow dung on the ground. That explained the smell. The cow had certainly given him a fright!

Buster and Chopper moved off toward the shed. Back to business!

6

The next morning, after he'd said good-bye to Ned and Aunt Tilly, Buster sneaked around the side of the house. He whistled quietly to Chopper. The dog appeared, wagging his tail.

"C'mon, boy. Let's go."

They raced off toward the orchard. Buster glanced over his shoulder to see if anyone was watching, but everything appeared quiet and still. They darted through the fruit trees and took a shortcut down to the road. When the house was out of sight, Buster slowed to a walk. His school-bag was heavy, but the thought of getting even with McGinty made it seem lighter.

At the bus stop, he dropped his bag with a clunk onto the ground. Chopper crouched in the dirt. It wasn't long before the school bus clattered around the bend. It stopped in front of them in a cloud of dust and fumes.

Chopper followed Buster up the steps. The

driver frowned and grunted, "No dogs allowed on the bus, son."

"He won't be any trouble," Buster replied anxiously.

"I said, out!"

The driver pointed at Chopper and the dog backed down onto the road. Buster hesitated on the top step. What would he do? He needed the dog at school with him.

"Well, don't just stand there, son. Make up your mind. Are you getting on or not?"

Buster turned and got off the bus. He'd just have to change his plan a bit. McGinty leaned out the back window as the bus took off.

"Cutting school today, Thompson? You'll be in trouble!"

"Get lost," shouted Buster, getting red in the face. He dragged his schoolbag back up to the orchard. The thick trees hid him from the house and road. Chopper sniffed at the bag.

He could smell the pudding!

Buster pulled out Chopper's goggles and fixed them over the dog's head. Next, he put on his leather flying helmet, followed by his magnificent disguise. He'd been up since dawn working on it.

Buster had cut two sections out of an old egg carton, made a hole in each side, tied the string through in a loop to fit over the back of his head, and made a small hole in the bottom of each eggcup so that he could see through them. When he pulled the homemade goggles over his eyes, nobody would recognize him!

With the disguise in place, it was time for THE PLAN! Buster removed a plastic two-liter fruit-juice container from his bag. It was three-quarters full, and heavy.

At school last night he'd collected water from a tin where the painters cleaned their brushes. The school buildings were being painted a cream color. The verandas, window frames, and doors were being painted red.

The water Buster had collected was bright red!

Chopper was pawing at a plastic bowl. He wanted the pudding. Buster removed the lid. The dog slurped eagerly and specks of yellow pudding flew everywhere.

"Here we go again!"

Chopper howled, his eyes turned red, and his tail started to spin around.

Buster quickly repacked his bag, slung it on his back, and jumped onboard the helicopter.

"To school!" he cried.

As they took off, Chopper swayed and sputtered, then adjusted to the extra weight. The ground fell away and Buster felt a lurch in the pit of his stomach. This was his first daytime flight. At night, he hadn't been able to see how far above the ground they were flying. He clutched at Chopper's collar. Everything looked so small down below.

Gradually he became used to the height. He relaxed and started to enjoy himself. It was a clear, sunny day and he could see for miles. Farmhouses looked like Lego blocks. Cows and sheep were dots in the paddocks, and tractors crawled about like Matchbox toys. He wondered what he looked like to the people down below.

When they approached the town, Buster went over the plan in his mind. He knew he'd have to act quickly. He reached into his backpack, pulled out the plastic bottle, and unscrewed the lid.

He was ready for action!

The school came into sight. Buster clung onto Chopper with his knees, holding the bottle in both hands. They circled high above the playground. Buster hoped the school bus had already arrived. He searched for McGinty through his goggles.

Yes! There he was!

"Down, boy!"

Chopper swooped in low.

All the children in the playground looked up at the sound of the approaching helicopter.

"What's that?"

"It's a flying saucer!"

"Not it's not. Flying saucers are round, dummy. It's a spaceship!"

"There's an alien on top."

"Look out! He's going to crash."

Boys and girls scattered in all directions. McGinty stood his ground. "I'm not afraid of aliens," he stated in a grand voice, arms folded across his chest.

Buster turned the bottle upside down.

Glug, glug . . . SPLASH!

McGinty was covered in huge red splotches.

"Aaah!" he screamed — an ear-piercing, ter- rified scream. "It's bleeding all over me. Get it off! Get it off!"

He brushed furiously at his clothes and hair. The more he rubbed, the further the paint spread.

"What's going on?" roared an angry voice.

Chopper and Buster, who had been circling above, disappeared in a flash behind the buildings. Mr. Baker had arrived to investigate the racket. McGinty was screaming his head off! The rest of the children stared at the school bully, their eyes almost popping out of their heads. Paint dripped down McGinty's face and into his mouth. As he screamed, red sparklers were spitting every- where!

"What's all this noise about?" demanded the principal. He stopped, astonished, in front of the red-striped apparition. Then he bellowed. "McGinty! I told the whole school that the paint was not to be touched!"

The children had never seen the principal so angry. His face was purple with rage.

"But, Sir. I didn't touch the paint," sobbed McGinty. "An alien flew in on a spaceship and bled all over me."

"You've gone too far this time, McGinty. You're suspended from school for one week! Stand over by the gate and DON'T MOVE. I'm going inside to call your mother. I don't want you dripping all over my carpet." The principal stormed back to his office.

McGinty shuffled over to the gate, muttering, "It was an alien. I saw it! I know an alien when I see one."

The others all started talking at the same time.

"Did you see it? It's head was cut off!"

"No it wasn't. There were huge eyes sticking out.

"It was a giant insect."

"Where did it go?"

"I didn't know aliens had red blood like humans."

Erin started to laugh. "Boy, did you see McGinty? He was really scared."

"His hair was as red as mine," grinned Danny. "I wonder if alien blood washes off. He might be red striped forever."

Just then the school bell rang. As everyone moved toward the classrooms, Buster stepped out from behind a building and joined the crowd. Danny was the only one who noticed.

7

At morning tea, all the children rushed outside to see if the alien had come back. McGinty had departed, dripping paint all over his mother's car. Buster searched the playground. Chopper was nowhere to be seen. The plan must have worked. He'd given him the last of the pudding before school began. He hoped it was enough to get the dog back to the farm.

Danny sauntered over. "I didn't see you get off the bus this morning, Buster."

"I was running late. I got a lift," he replied.

One of the boys from McGinty's gang went past. He was tall and strong, with long dangling arms like a gorilla. His hair stuck straight out over his eyes like a veranda. The other kids called him the Mean Machine.

"I bet you had something to do with McGinty and the alien," he growled. "I'll be watching you, Thompson."

Buster decided that it was wiser not to reply.

Danny looked at Buster. He was about to say something then changed his mind. Did Danny know?

Everyone was talking about Mr. Baker suspending the school bully.

"Serves him right."

"Maybe now he won't pick on everybody all the time."

"Did you see his face? It's the first time I've ever seen him scared."

Buster almost felt sorry for McGinty. During lunch, Erin came up to him in the playgound. "Are you going to the school dance tonight?" she asked.

Buster blushed. "Maybe," he muttered.

"Do you want to come with me?" she asked with a cheeky grin.

Buster was embarrassed. She seemed okay — for a girl. And she was a good cricket player. But he didn't want to go to the dance with her. Imagine what the other boys would say. He looked at his feet and scuffed his shoes in the dirt. He didn't answer.

"Don't you like talking to girls?" she persisted. "Do you have any sisters?"

"No."

"Well you must talk to your mother."

"I don't have a mother," he stated defiantly.

Erin was shocked. Everyone she knew had a mother. She didn't know what to say. There was silence.

"Who do you live with?" she tried.

Buster had a lump in his throat. He swallowed hard a couple of times. When he spoke, his voice sounded scratchy. "I'm staying with Ned and my Great-aunt Tilly. Dad's gone to Sweden."

Erin wasn't exactly sure where Sweden was, but she knew it was far away on the other side of the world. Somewhere near the North Pole, she thought.

"Do you have a brother?"

"No, there's just me."

Erin tried to imagine being all by herself. It must be very lonely. She wondered where Buster's mother was.

As if reading her mind, Buster blurted out, "Mom's dead."

Then he wished he hadn't said anything. Now the whole school would know.

Erin could see that Buster was upset.

"I won't tell anybody if you don't want me to," she offered.

Buster walked away. He plunked himself down on a low brick wall surrounding the basketball court. Erin hesitated, then followed. Suddenly Buster found himself telling her how his mother had died from cancer. How terrible it was on Mother's Day not to have a mother. How much he missed her when he came home from school and she wasn't there.

"Mom used to ask me all about my day. Dad's

always cranky when he comes in from work. He rushes around getting dinner and shouting at me to get on with my homework. We used to have fun together. Since Mom died, everything's changed."

He squeezed his eyes shut. He was *not* going to cry. Especially in front of a girl.

"My dad yells at me when I don't eat my vegetables. Says I should think of all the starving children in the world. I'd be happy to send them a package every week — especially the brussels sprouts!" said Erin.

They both laughed. Buster felt better. It was the first time he'd talked with anyone about his mom dying.

The school bell rang. They stood up and moved off together. Buster said casually, "Might see you at the dance tonight."

"Sure." Erin smiled.

Buster jumped off the bus after school and raced up the track to the farmhouse. He had to find Chopper. Had the dog arrived back safely? He called and whistled, but there was no answering bark.

He burst through the kitchen door flung his schoolbag down, and fell into a chair, panting.

Aunt Tilly looked up, startled. She was spreading chocolate icing on a cake.

"Goodness. You're in a hurry," she said.

"Have you seen Chopper?" he puffed.

"Not for a while. Oh, that's right. Ned took him out on the motorbike. They're moving sheep. Would you like a piece of cake or a cookie?"

Buster's grin threatened to split his face. His secret was safe. And so was Chopper. "I'd love a piece of cake. Actually, you're a pretty good cook, Aunt Tilly. Almost as good as Mom was."

Aunt Tilly glanced at Buster. She hadn't heard him talk about his mother before. "You seem very pleased with yourself this afternoon. Had a good day at school, have you?"

"It was great!" he replied.

"Well, I'm glad you haven't been fighting again with that boy, what's his name?"

"McGinty."

"Yes. Well, fighting doesn't solve anything. If you have a problem, you should talk about it. Are you getting along better with McGinty now?"

Buster was saved from answering by the roar of the motorbike. Ned and Chopper were back. Later when no one was around, he'd have to empty his schoolbag and wash out the juice and pudding containers.

He rushed outside, glad to escape Aunt Tilly's questions. Chopper jumped off the bike, barking excitedly. Buster hugged him tight.

"You two appear happy to see each other," said

Ned as they went into the kitchen. "That's the first time all afternoon I've seen Chopper with any energy. Can't imagine why he's been so tired."

Did Ned have a twinkle in his eye? Buster looked at the dog. He could have sworn Chopper winked at him.

8

After tea, Ned drove Buster to the school dance. As they pulled up next to a group of cars, loud music blasted out at them. Flashing lights winked through the windows of the school hall, like a Christmas tree gone crazy.

Buster was nervous. He hoped Danny had arrived.

"See you at nine o'clock," said Ned as Buster climbed down from the truck.

Danny was waiting just inside the door. A group of children were already dancing and the floor pounded with the beat of their feet. It was dark inside except for the colored lights, which flashed on and off in time to the music, lighting up one section, then another.

"I'm glad you decided to come," Danny shouted into Buster's ear, above the blaring music.

They moved toward the back of the hall. Everybody seemed to be dancing in one large group. That was a relief. Maybe you didn't have to ask the girls to dance. It wasn't long before Buster's feet were tapping to the beat.

"Come on." Danny pulled him toward the dancers.

At first, Buster felt self-conscious. He was sure the others were looking at him, but after a while he relaxed. Everyone was too busy enjoying themselves to stare at him.

The hall filled up rapidly as more and more children arrived. The deejay started a dance competition and Buster found himself dancing next to Erin.

"Hi," she shouted, her blond hair flying wildly from side to side, free from its daytime braids.

Buster had never seen her out of school uniform before. She looked stunning in a hot-pink, short skirt and pink-and-black spotted shirt. He tried to think of something clever to say, but couldn't. It didn't matter anyway. The music was too loud to carry on a conversation. Maybe she'd be impressed by his dancing. He tried out some fancy steps he'd seen on a rock video. Not bad, he thought as Erin grinned.

What a great night! Dancing, drinks, ice cream and more dancing. When the deejay announced the last song, a roar echoed around the hall.

"More, more, we want more!"

The floor vibrated as dozens of feet stamped in rhythm to the chanting. One of the mothers who had helped organize the evening made an announcement, "There'll be another dance next month!"

A roar of approval threatened to lift the roof off.

"I wish I could go to school here all the time," Buster said to Danny as they went outside.

"Why don't you ask your dad?" Danny replied as his mother came over to them.

"Hello, Buster. I've just been talking to Ned. I asked him if you'd be allowed to have a sleepover at our house next weekend."

"Great. Thanks, Mrs. Morgan. What did he say?"

"Ned is going to check with your Aunt Tilly. You can let Danny know on Monday at school," Mrs. Morgan said.

"Make sure she says yes," said Danny over his shoulder as they moved toward their car.

"See you Monday, Buster," called Erin as she walked past.

"Friend of yours?" Ned asked as Buster climbed into the truck.

"Just a girl from my class," he mumbled.

Ned smirked. "Did you have a good time?"

"It was great! I wish I could stay here," he added in a rush.

Ned reached across and patted his shoulder.

When they got home, Aunt Tilly fussed around, made hot drinks, and cut large slabs of chocolate cake smothered in red cherries. She wanted to know all about the dance. Buster repeated what he'd told Ned, in between mouthfuls of cake. When he started yawning, Aunt Tilly shooed him off to bed.

Buster thought back over the day and evening. He could never have imagined how much fun it would be staying at the farm. The problem with McGinty had been sorted out and he'd made some good friends. He stroked Chopper's head. The dog slept on the bed with him every night now. Buster fell asleep wondering whether or not he would tell Danny about Chopper and the pudding.

On Monday, Danny was thrilled to hear that Aunt Tilly had said yes to the sleepover. Peace reigned at school all week without McGinty. Danny and Buster spent every spare moment planning. "Why don't we have a midnight feast on Saturday night?" Danny suggested. "We can save cake and cookies from morning and afternoon tea during the week and hide them until the weekend."

"That's a great idea," agreed Buster.

"I've got some allowance saved," Danny continued. "I could buy some lollipops at the corner shop and hide them in my bedside drawer."

"Won't your mom find them?"

"No. She says she's sick and tired of cleaning my room. Calls it 'Danny's Dump!' I have to clean my own room now. But don't tell the twins about the feast. They'll tell Mom. You know what little sisters are like," Danny moaned.

The twins were eight years old and Danny was always complaining about them. Double trouble, he said, and called them The Pests! Pest One and Pest Two.

"We'll have to be very quiet when we get up in the night, otherwise Snowy will wake up," Danny went on.

"Who's Snowy?"

"He's our pet cockatoo."

"Can he talk?"

"Sure can. Never shuts up. Even swears sometimes."

Buster laughed. "Where did you get him?"

"He used to belong to Mom's brother. When Uncle Bill moved to New Zealand, he asked Mom to look after Snowy. He really shocks Mom's friends sometimes. Mom's tried putting his cage out in the garage, but he just screeches even louder!"

The two boys roared with laughter. The planning continued.

Buster managed to save quite a lot of food during the week. He found a crumpled, brown paper bag containing half a moldy sandwich in his backpack. He threw the old lunch away and used the bag to store cookies in. At afternoon tea each day when Aunt Tilly wasn't looking, he'd slip a cookie into his pocket instead of eating it. He kept the bag in the bottom of his wardrobe. Sometimes he'd forget it was there and throw his shoes on top of it, breaking the cookies. Some of the pieces were still quite large though, so he was sure they'd taste just as good.

He'd also saved a banana. It was too large to fit in the bag with the cookies, so he hid it in his coat pocket. His coat hung on a hook behind the door and several times he'd caught Chopper sniffing around it.

Danny said he'd bought the lollipops and they were safely stored in his bedside drawer. He'd also saved a couple of pieces of cake and had hidden them in an old chalk tin. Between the two of them, they should have plenty of food for the feast.

9

Saturday finally arrived.

"I'll drive you over to the Morgans', Buster. I want to get a few things in town on the way," Aunt Tilly said.

She had offered to help pack Buster's overnight bag, but he said he'd rather do it himself. He'd hidden the bag of cookie pieces underneath his pajamas.

"Don't forget to take your coat," Aunt Tilly called up the stairs.

"I won't," replied Buster. He stuffed it into the top of his bag.

Buster went downstairs and waited for Aunt Tilly to bring the truck around. She seemed to take forever, so he sat down on his bag. He completely forgot about the banana. The bag sagged under him.

The truck kangarooed to a halt. Buster climbed in and they were off. He hoped he wouldn't see any kids from school when they drove through the town. Aunt Tilly was still crunching the gears! How embarrassing!

When they reached the main street he pulled his hat over his eyes and slid down in the seat. With a bit of luck nobody would recognize him. Aunt Tilly made a couple of stops, kangarooing the truck each time she took off in first gear. Buster stared straight at the floor, not daring to look out of the window. He was *so* relieved when they reached the Morgans'.

Danny rushed out. "Hi. I thought you'd never get here. I've been up for hours."

The two boys ran inside while the women talked.

"Did you remember to bring the food for the feast?" Danny asked as he showed Buster his room.

"Sure did. And look at this!" Buster dragged his precious skeleton out of the bag.

Danny examined the cow's head with great interest. "Where did you get it?"

"From Aunt Tilly's woodshed. It's got heaps of great stuff in it. I found this old war helmet, too," Buster answered. He pulled out the tin hat with a flourish.

"We could use these to scare The Pests tonight," Danny said thoughtfully.

He scrabbled around in one of his drawers and found a small flashlight, then held it up inside the cow's head and turned it on. The skeleton's empty eye sockets lit up — huge, round, and yellow. Gross!

"It'll look even more revolting in the dark," laughed Danny.

Buster perched the tin hat on the cow's head. Both boys collapsed onto the bed, shrieking with laughter.

There was a knock on the bedroom door and Mrs. Morgan called, "Would you like some morning tea?"

Danny quickly pushed the apparition under the bed just as the door opened.

"You two sound like you're having a good time. Buster, I'll bring a folding bed in here tonight for you to sleep on. Do you have anything in your bag that needs to be hung up?"

"Only my coat," replied Buster.

He jumped up off the bed, only to discover that his coat had been underneath him. He felt the pocket cautiously. It seemed a bit squishy, but he'd have to check it later when Mrs. Morgan wasn't around.

"Hang it up with Danny's behind the door," said Mrs. Morgan, "and then come into the kitchen."

They had a great day. Luckily, there was a spare bike, so they were able to go riding together. Danny took Buster to all his favorite places and they rode for hours.

On the way home, they clattered over the

wooden bridge that crossed the river. Danny skidded to an abrupt halt. "Look who's down there. It's McGinty!"

Sure enough, it was McGinty rowing downstream in a small boat.

"Hey, McGinty!" Danny yelled. "Look out for the aliens!"

"Get out of here," came the shouted reply. The school bully stood up in the rowboat and shook his oar at them. The boat started to wobble dangerously, then tipped. McGinty and the oar were flung into the muddy brown water with a massive splash!

"What a stupid thing to do," scoffed Buster. "Everybody knows you never stand up in a small boat."

Danny laughed. "McGinty isn't as smart as he thinks he is."

They peered over the side of the bridge. McGinty's head appeared out of the water and his arms started to thrash around frantically. His head went under the water. A couple of seconds later it appeared again.

"Do you think he can swim?" Buster asked Danny.

"Of course he can. He's just fooling around," Danny replied.

McGinty's head disappeared from sight again, then resurfaced. His arms appeared tired as he continued to flail at the water.

"Danny! I think he's drowning. Come on!"

They raced along the bridge and down to the riverbank.

"What are you going to do?" cried Danny.

"Rescue him, of course!"

Buster peeled off his shoes and socks and waded into the water. He quickly set off downstream in his best freestyle stroke. Danny watched from the bank, openmouthed. Buster was a fantastic swimmer!

McGinty's head appeared yet again, minus the arms this time, then sank quietly from view. Buster had almost reached the spot where McGinty had disappeared. He stopped swimming and looked around.

"Where is he?" he yelled.

Danny ran along the bank. "He went down just near you. You'll have to dive for him."

Buster did a duck-dive and also disappeared. Danny's heart was pounding. Why had he called out to McGinty in the first place? What if he drowned? What if Buster drowned, too? Come on, Buster, hurry up! Where are you?

The seconds ticked by.

Buster's head burst out of the water, followed by McGinty's. They started to move toward the riverbank and Danny saw that Buster and McGinty were on their backs. Buster appeared to be pulling McGinty along by his chin. Danny waded into the river to meet them.

"He's unconscious!" Buster gasped.

Danny grabbed McGinty under the arms as Buster struggled to stand up. Between the two of them, they dragged McGinty out of the water and dumped him on the muddy bank.

"Quick! Turn him on his side. He's probably swallowed a lot of water," Buster puffed as he collapsed, exhausted, beside the body.

Danny pushed and shoved and managed to roll McGinty onto his side. He didn't seem to be breathing.

"Hit him on the back," croaked Buster.

Thump. Thump.

With a whoosh, a dirty stream of water shot out of McGinty's mouth and sprayed all over Buster. McGinty coughed and coughed and his body jerked violently with the effort. Water streamed from his eyes and nose as he lifted one hand weakly to brush it away. Buster lay panting beside him.

"What happened?" spluttered McGinty.

"You fell out of the boat, you idiot," Danny said angrily. "Buster might have drowned trying to rescue you."

There was no answer for a minute or two, only the sound of the two boys struggling to catch their breaths.

"You're lucky Buster's such a good swimmer."

"Aw, cool it, Danny," said Buster. "It's okay."

"Well, it's true. If you hadn't been here he

would have drowned!" Danny wasn't giving up easily.

"And if you hadn't been here, it would never have happened at all," McGinty snapped.

"Forget it, you two. It's over," Buster stated.

McGinty sat up. "You're not so bad — for a city kid," McGinty offered grudgingly. "I guess I owe you one, Buster."

10

The boys were starving when they eventually arrived home. Mr. Morgan cooked hamburgers on the barbecue for tea. "How many can you eat, Buster?" he asked.

"Three'll do me," he replied. He was ravenous after rescuing McGinty, but he wanted to leave room for the midnight feast.

The twins and Danny all seemed to talk at once over their meal.

"You have to speak loudly if you want to be heard at this table," Mr. Morgan smiled at Buster. "I suppose it's a bit noisier than you're used to."

"I don't mind."

Actually, despite the arguments, it seemed sort of friendly. Buster wished he had a brother to argue with!

After tea they watched a video, then went to Danny's room to make their plans.

Danny's mom came in to say good night and

turn off the light. "You can talk quietly for a while, but please don't disturb the girls," she said.

They whispered and giggled together for ages, then Danny said, "Come on. Let's go and frighten The Pests!"

They crept out of bed. Danny's parents were still watching television in the living room. Buster could just hear the faint wail of a siren. Maybe it was a police show. Danny turned his flashlight on and retrieved the cow's head and tin hat from under the bed.

"Push the window right up," he whispered.

Buster pushed it up slowly, carefully. Squeeeak!

The boys froze. Danny snapped the flashlight off! Nobody came. He switched the flashlight back on. "You climb out first and I'll pass everything to you."

Buster swung one leg over the windowsill and pulled himself up. He balanced in the open window for a moment then jumped to the ground with a soft thud. Danny passed the things down to him and followed.

The grass was damp under their bare feet. They crept along in the dark to the girls' bedroom window.

"Can you wail like a ghost?" Danny whispered to Buster.

"I'll try."

"Wait a minute."

Danny broke a stick off a nearby gum tree and tapped on the girls' window. Tap, tap, tap . . . tap, tap, tap.

"What was that?" came a whisper. "Melanie, are you awake?"

"What's the matter," a sleepy voice replied.

"I heard something outside. Listen!"

Danny dug Buster in the ribs and he started to moan quietly. "A a a h . . . a a h." Buster tried not to look at Danny because he knew he'd start to laugh. He moaned a bit louder. "A a a a h . . . a a a h!"

Danny turned on the flashlight, placed it inside the skull, and stuck the helmet on top. He poked it in through the open window. Buster groaned louder.

The girls screamed!

The boys fled back to their window and clambered through. In his haste, Danny tripped and fell to the floor. Buster hauled him up and they raced to their beds, shoving the "ghost" out of sight. Buster could feel wet grass sticking to his feet as he pulled the bedclothes over his head.

Danny buried his face under the pillow and tried to muffle his laughter. His shoulders shook.

The girls were still screaming and Buster could hear their parents speaking.

"What happened?"

"What's the matter?"

"A ghost! At the window," sobbed Melanie. "It was horrible."

"I'm sure it wasn't a ghost," soothed Mrs. Morgan. "It was probably just the moon shining through the curtains."

"No. It was a ghost," cried Amelia. "I saw its head. It was groaning."

"Now, now, I think you've both been dreaming," said their mother. "Settle down or you'll wake the boys."

Footsteps came toward Danny's room. The door opened gently. Buster tried to breathe slowly as if he was asleep. He held the blankets tight around his head. The door closed again.

Danny had been holding his breath, trying not to laugh. He let out a gasp as the footsteps faded away.

"I couldn't have held my breath any longer," he whispered. They could hear Danny's parents still trying to calm the girls. Gradually, the noise subsided and all was quiet.

Buster was tired. It had been a hectic day. "How will we know when it's midnight?" he whispered.

"I'm sure I'll just wake up," replied Danny.

It wasn't long before they were both asleep.

Next thing Buster knew, Danny was shaking him.

"Buster, wake up! It's time for the feast."

He sat up and rubbed his eyes. Danny switched on the flashlight and opened the bottom drawer of the bedside table. A trail of ants stretched right through the lollipops!

They both stared in dismay. All the multi-colored sweets were covered in little black specks.

"I know. I'll wash the ants off in the bathroom. You get your things out while I'm gone," said Danny.

Buster opened the door silently for him and Danny crept down the hallway, hands full of wriggling lollipops.

"I can hear you! I can hear you!" screeched Snowy.

"Shut up!" hissed Danny.

A muffled squawk followed, then silence.

Buster waited to see if anyone woke up. Not a sound. That was close! With the light from the flashlight he found the bag of cookies. He tore down one side and opened the bag to make a plate, then fished around in his coat pocket for the banana. His hand filled with a soggy mess. He pulled it out and tried to push some of the runny bits back inside the split skin.

Danny sneaked back in and shut the door. Colored streaks ran down his arms. Red, yellow, green — all mixed together and covered with bits of chocolate. "I got the ants off all right, but some of the color has run out," he grinned. "What have you got?"

Buster licked his fingers. "Cookies and a banana. The banana's a bit squashed, but it tastes okay."

Danny took the chalk tin out of his cupboard and tipped the cake out into his school hat. "Have some," he offered.

It tasted a bit gritty, mixed with chalk dust, but the tin had kept it reasonably fresh. The cookies were stale, but there was a good variety of them.

What a night!

And they still had one more day together. Buster wished the weekend would last forever.

11

Buster raced downstairs to answer the telephone. It had been pouring with rain all week. Now, on Friday afternoon, a watery sun had finally appeared. Aunt Tilly took advantage of the break in the weather to drive into town and collect supplies. Ned was moving sheep to drier ground.

"Hello."

"It's Mrs. Morgan speaking. Is that you, Buster?"

"Yep."

"Is Danny with you?"

"No, I haven't seen him since we left school this afternoon."

"If he turns up, could you ask him to call me, please?" Mrs. Morgan sounded worried. "We had a bit of an argument and he stormed off in a rage. It's almost teatime. He's been gone for ages."

She sounded as though she might start crying. "I've checked all his usual hiding places, but I can't find him anywhere. If he doesn't come home soon, I might have to call the police."

"I bet he'll be back for his tea," laughed Buster. "You know how Danny loves eating."

"You *will* call me if he arrives at your place, won't you?"

"Sure thing, Mrs. Morgan."

"Thanks, Buster."

The phone clicked.

He wandered into the kitchen. Where would Danny go? Somewhere that nobody would find him.

The old orchard! That was it. Danny's thinking place. He'd taken Buster there last weekend and sworn him to secrecy. Better go and check, before Mrs. Morgan called the police. Danny would have a fit if they came looking for him!

It was a fair hike from Aunt Tilly's, though. It would have to be the helicopter!

He checked the fridge. Sure enough, a bowl of pudding sat there, staring back at him. A big, yellow moon face.

Buster raced upstairs to get the helmet and goggles.

"Chopper, Chopper!"

Ned had told the dog to stay with Buster while he and Aunt Tilly were out. By the time Buster ran back into the kitchen, Chopper was standing beside the fridge. He knew!

"Come on. Let's find Danny."

And they were off, whirring along through the late afternoon sky, Buster in his leather flying helmet and Chopper wearing the goggles. The dog looked hilarious, with its ears flattened against its head by the goggles strap.

In the distance, a mob of sheep were being moved steadily along by a motorbike. Was that Ned? Would he notice? After about ten minutes, Buster spotted a derelict farmhouse and the old orchard. He pointed downward and Chopper cruised in to a landing. Thump!

"Where's Danny? Find Danny."

The dog sniffed around the fruit trees — tail up, head down. Buster clambered through the remains of the house. It must be a long time since anybody had lived in it. Part of the roof had fallen in and the rooms were festooned with cobwebs. What if a ghost lived here? The hair on the back of his neck stood up.

"Daaannnnny. Danny!" he called urgently.

No answer.

Wind whistled eerily through the broken windows. It was spooky!

Chopper barked.

The sudden noise made Buster jump. He hurried outside, glad to be out in the open, and was just in time to see Chopper tearing off through the trees — nose to the ground. He'd found a scent. Buster took off after him. "Wait for me!"

An overgrown track led through thick scrub.

Blackberry vines scratched and pulled at his clothes and skin and tried to hold him back. He held his arms up in front of him to protect his face.

And just as suddenly as he'd entered the bush, he was out of it — in a clearing. Chopper was sniffing around over on the far side.

Chopper suddenly disappeared.

"Wait, don't leave me," hollered Buster. He ran over to where the dog had vanished and pushed his way into the bush again. He pulled up sharply, heart pounding, hands clutching at branches, his toes on the edge of a cliff! He'd almost stepped right off! The split in the earth had been completely hidden. Sweat poured down his face and body and he moved backward quickly. His legs shook with fright.

"Chopper!"

An excited bark sounded from away to the left. Buster sighed with relief. Thank goodness Chopper hadn't fallen over. He was just hidden.

Buster plucked up enough courage to peer over the cliff. His stomach lurched! It was a long way to the bottom. A waterfall splashed down over shiny black boulders.

Chopper pushed his way back under some bushes to reach Buster. The dog barked and barked, its two feet planted right on the edge.

Buster grabbed the dog's collar. "Come back, you'll fall."

"Danny, are you down there?" he called anxiously.

No answer.

"DANNY!" he yelled, in a louder voice this time. Gingerly, he moved further along and called again. "Coo . . . ee. Coo . . . ee!"

The sound echoed around him. He listened intently. Was that a voice?

"Quiet, Chopper." He listened again.

"Help," came a faint cry over the noise of running water.

"Danny! Are you okay?"

"My leg. I think it's broken."

"Hang on. I'll get you out of there," Buster shouted.

He pushed shrubs out of his way and moved sideways along the edge as he tried to see his friend. Suddenly, one foot slipped from under him as the ground crumbled away. He grabbed frantically at the bushes. Stones and dirt flew through the air and landed on the rocks below. Buster ended up sitting on his bottom — legs dangling into space. His heart raced like an express train. His stomach felt as if it had jumped into his mouth.

"Whew!" he gasped. "That was close!" He sat perfectly still, not daring to move. The ground was wet and slippery after the torrential rain during the week. Part of the edge of the cliff had broken away. That must be how Danny had fallen. It was a long way down.

Buster looked around. He might be able to reach Danny if he was very careful, but how would he get him back up the cliff if his leg was broken? And it would be dark soon. Buster made a decision.

"Danny. I'll have to get help," he called.

"Don't leave me."

His friend sounded weak and frightened.

"Chopper will wait here with you. Don't worry. I'll be back soon."

Buster was feeling scared himself, but he didn't want Danny to know.

"Stay, Chopper," he commanded. The dog crouched down and whimpered.

"Stay!" Buster repeated.

He looked over his shoulder and tried to remember which way he'd come. If only Chopper could come with him. He took a deep breath, stood up slowly, and didn't dare look down. His feet dislodged a few more stones.

Crash, rumble . . . plop!

They hit the water below. Buster jumped backward in fright. He wouldn't be any use to Danny if he fell over, too. "Come on," he told himself. "Get going." He bent down and patted Chopper's head. "Good boy. Stay," he whispered, then pushed his way through the bush and back into the clearing.

Where was the track? He looked around. Which way had they come? He didn't know. What if he was lost?

"Stop it!" he told himself. "Don't panic. Think!"

Footprints. That was it. The ground was wet, there must be footprints. He searched carefully among the leaves. Hooray! He found some of Chopper's paw prints dotted across the clearing.

There was the entrance to the track, partially hidden by an overhanging banksia tree.

Once on the overgrown path, the way became easier, but the sun was already setting behind the hill.

He seemed to walk forever. Surely it hadn't been this far? What if he'd taken a wrong turn? Perhaps when he'd crossed the log a few moments before, he should have taken that smaller track.

He hesitated, looked behind, then forward again. No, he'd keep going. For a bit longer, anyway.

Overhead, a white cockatoo screeched, startling him.

Splat!

Something landed beside him and splattered his jeans. A rotten apple! A disgusting, sloppy, rotten apple! He shook his fist at the bird perched in a tree above him.

Wait a minute!

He grinned. "You little beauty!" he yelled in delight.

He must be close to the orchard! He pushed on eagerly. At last, there was the old farmhouse right in front of him. But now what? He still had a long way to go before he reached help. Too long. He didn't want to become lost in the dark.

Exhausted, he sat on the ground. He should never have come out here looking for Danny in the first place.

Don't think like that, he thought — do something!

An idea came to him. An idea so simple, he wondered why he hadn't thought of it earlier. It had to work. He didn't dare think what might happen to Danny otherwise.

He raced over to the old swing, hanging sadly from a forgotten apple tree.

12

It was almost dark when Buster found his way back to Chopper. He hugged the dog tightly.

"Danny, I'm here." His voice echoed around the cliffs.

Silence.

"Daaannnny. Danny! Are you okay?"

Still no answer.

Buster hoped that Chopper had enough fuel to complete the rescue plan. He moved along the edge of the cliff until he found a place that was almost clear of bush. He draped the rope from the swing over his head and across one shoulder, then climbed onto Chopper's back.

"Down. Go down! Find Danny."

Buster held his breath. For a moment nothing happened. Then a faint whirr, followed by a full throated roar as they took off.

They hovered over the waterfall, then moved lower, slowly, searching for Danny. And there he was, lying crumpled and still like a rag doll, just to the side of the waterfall.

Chopper landed on the shiny black rocks. Spray misted over them like a damp blanket. Danny didn't move. He just lay there with his eyes shut.

Buster was petrified. He knelt down and put his ear to Danny's chest. He'd seen someone do that once in a movie, to check if a person was still alive.

Boom, boom. Boom, boom. Boom, boom.

For a moment the noise startled him, then he realized that it was Danny's heartbeat. Thank goodness he was still alive. He must have fainted.

"Danny, wake up. It's me."

There was a faint moan. Danny opened his eyes and stared at Buster in a daze.

"Where am I? My leg hurts."

For the first time, Buster looked at Danny's legs. The right one was sticking out from his body at a funny angle. It had a strange bulge on the top half.

"Can you move your leg?" Buster asked.

Danny tried and screamed. Tears ran down his face. "It hurts, it hurts," he sobbed.

Buster stood up and lifted the rope over his head. Luckily, Danny had landed on a strip of grass beside the waterfall. It was quite soft because the spray kept the ground damp, but slippery rocks were on either side.

"I'm going to tie this rope around you and get Chopper to fly you out," said Buster.

"What?" Danny asked, a bewildered look on his face.

"Don't worry. Just stay very still and you'll be all right."

Buster busied himself with the rope, pushing one end under Danny's arms and around his body. By the time he had finished, his friend looked like a Christmas turkey all trussed up for the oven. He tied the other end to Chopper's collar, fumbling with the knot. Buster's hands were shaking. He hoped the rope would hold.

Danny didn't say a word. His face was chalk-white and his body was deathly cold. He didn't seem to really know what was going on.

"Okay. We're all set." Buster tried to sound cheerful and unconcerned.

Danny's eyelids fluttered, and then shut.

"Up, Chopper, up," Buster urged.

The dog looked exhausted, but managed to lift off slowly, slowly, toward the sky. He was losing strength and Buster began to panic.

"Keep going, keep going," he yelled.

Danny was swinging crazily from side to side. Chopper's engine sounded like a sick lawnmower. The dog had to fly higher than the cliff top so that he could lower the injured boy to the ground. Finally he managed it, and then dropped to the cliff edge himself with a sickening thud. There was no sound from Danny.

Chopper barked.

"Danny, untie the rope," called Buster.

No reply.

He began to feel angry. Danny was supposed to undo the rope and drop it back down to him. Now how was *he* going to get back up the cliff? He'd gone to all the trouble of rescuing his friend and now he was trapped himself.

Buster looked around. Night was closing in rapidly, and it was creepy. There was only the sound of falling water, and Chopper barking at the top of the cliff. Thick clouds raced across the darkening sky.

Was it going to rain again? That's all he'd need. A whole lot more water pouring down trying to wash him away.

"Do something, Chopper. Don't just stand there barking," he shouted angrily.

Silence. Except for the sound of the waterfall.

Buster waited. He peered up through the gloom. What was happening?

Screech, screech, screech!

A black shadow whizzed past his head with a high-pitched squawk. He nearly jumped out of his skin. The air around him filled with flapping and whirring sounds. Buster crouched down, terrified, hands over his ears, as the black mass passed over

87

him. Bats! He'd never seen so many that close before. They probably fed on the old fruit trees in the orchard.

"CHOPPER!" he hollered.

The dog barked.

A slithering sound came down the cliff. Buster froze. A snake? With relief, he saw the rope appear. He leaned precariously over the waterfall and tried to grab the end of the rope. His hand couldn't reach it. Slowly, he inched forward onto the shiny boulder beside him, his feet slipping and sliding.

Swipe! He had it

Yuk! The end of the rope was frayed, with saliva slobbered all over it. Chopper must have chewed through Danny's end, then dropped it down to Buster. He wiped his hands down his jeans, one at a time. He didn't dare let go of the rope completely, in case he lost it.

Cautiously he moved back to the grass where it was safe, then pulled on the rope. The other end, he hoped, was still attached to Chopper's collar. There had been no sound from Danny, and Chopper was out of fuel. There was only one thing to do. He'd have to climb back up the cliff.

Buster tied the rope around his waist in case he fell, and called, "Brace yourself, Chopper! I'm coming up."

He felt the damp rocks above him, searching for hand- and footholds, and started slowly up the cliff face. There was no light left now and Buster could hardly see where he was going. His heart thudded against his ribs. One hand grabbed at a rocky outcrop.

Whack!

A clod of dirt hit him in the face and rocks crashed down around him. He ducked his head, then found himself sliding backward in a shower of earth and stones.

"Blast it!" he yelled, as he landed on his bottom. Angry and frustrated, he spat dirt out of his mouth. It was no good. He'd never make it. Especially at night.

Chopper's bark echoed eerily. Buster couldn't see him now. It was very lonely down here. He shivered — cold, wet, and frightened.

Would anybody ever find him, stranded at the bottom of the waterfall? And what about Danny? Was he going to die?

Chopper couldn't fly without more pudding. Why didn't he think to bring extra fuel?

"Don't be stupid," he told himself sternly. "Stop thinking about bad things. There has to be a way."

Of course! Chopper can't fly, but he can still walk.

It was a long way back to the farm and the dog was exhausted. But he'd heard stories of dogs who'd walked hundreds of miles when they were sick or injured. Surely Chopper could do it.

"Chew through the rope, Chopper," Buster called.

He untied his end. The barking stopped. Buster waited anxiously. It seemed forever before the rope crashed down and landed at his feet.

"Get help, Chopper. Fetch Ned!"

The dog whimpered.

"Go!" he shouted. "Now!"

Buster listened. Water gurgled beside him. He couldn't hear Chopper. I hope he makes it, he thought.

Buster's stomach growled, which reminded him that it was way past teatime. Surely by now somebody would wonder where he was? There was nothing to do but wait.

13

Hours passed. Or so it seemed. Buster sat with his arms huddled around his knees, trying to warm himself. His teeth chattered as he burrowed his head deep against his chest. Moisture seeped into his clothes and his bones ached with the cold.

He tried not to think about food, but pictures kept flashing into his mind. Apple pie and ice cream. Crisp baked potatoes and the crunchy outside slices of a roast leg of lamb. A big juicy hamburger. He was so hungry he could probably even eat pudding! He licked his lips.

Aunt Tilly and Ned must be looking for him by now. There hadn't been a sound from Danny. Probably just as well. If he woke up in the dark, he could easily fall over the cliff again. Buster told himself that his best friend was still alive. He had to be. I've never had a friend like Danny before, he thought, and I'm not going to lose him now.

The night pressed in around him. Strange as it might seem, he was actually getting used to the dark. But he wished someone would hurry up and rescue him. Memories of his mother floated into his head. He still missed her terribly, but it had been great fun staying at the farm. He'd had some fabulous adventures.

I wonder what Dad's doing now? I hope he comes back soon, he thought, as he drifted off to sleep.

"B u s t e r . . . B u s t e r . . ."
He dreamed that Aunt Tilly was calling him for dinner. What would it be tonight? Spaghetti Bolognese?

"Buster . . . Buster!"
The voice became more insistent. In fact there was more than one voice. Buster woke with a start. Where was he? He couldn't see anything. Then he remembered. At the bottom of a cliff! And he wasn't being called for dinner.

"Down here," he yelled. "Beside the waterfall."
Lights flashed above him and there was the sound of feet thrashing through the undergrowth.

"Sounds like they've brought in the army," Buster said to himself.

A spotlight flashed over him as he screwed up his eyes.

"There he is! On the rock."
"Don't move! We'll get you up," a voice called.
"Danny's hurt. Up there. Have you found him?" Buster shouted.

There was more crashing and Buster heard a faint voice.

"Here he is. Looks serious. Bring a blanket."

The next couple of hours passed in a haze. Buster remembered being strapped to a man and hauled up the cliff face, then being carried through the bush and Chopper licking his hand. A vague memory of bumping along in Ned's truck and Aunt Tilly exclaiming over his cuts and bruises settled in the back of his mind. Next thing he knew, he was sinking down into his big bed at the farm. It was so warm and comfortable. . . .

Something wet touched Buster's hand. He opened his eyes slowly. Chopper was there, tail wagging and a grin from ear to ear.

Buster gave a weak smile and patted the dog's head.

"I knew you could do it, Chopper," he whispered.

"How are you feeling?" came a deep voice from a corner of the room.

Startled, Buster turned his head. "Dad! What are you doing here?"

"I've come to take you home."

"What? Now?"

"No, when you're feeling better. Just rest and go back to sleep."

Suddenly, Buster remembered his friend. He

struggled to sit up. "Danny! Where's Danny? Is he all right?"

His father moved the chair closer to Buster's bed.

"Take it easy. Settle down. The doctors think he's going to be okay. His leg is badly broken and he's suffering from shock. He'll be in the hospital for quite a while. You can go and see him when you recover."

"When did you get here?" Buster asked, puzzled. He lay back on the pillow.

"This afternoon. I wanted to surprise you. Aunt Tilly picked me up at the railway station when she came in for supplies. When we got to the farm, you were gone. Chopper eventually turned up and led the search party back to you. He's a mighty fine dog!"

Chopper thumped his tail on the floor.

"You wouldn't believe how fantastic he is, Dad!"

"Go back to sleep now. We'll talk about it in the morning," his father said and hugged him.

"I'm glad you're here, Dad. Don't go away again," Buster replied sleepily.

"I needed to be by myself for a while. It's been hard for me since your mother died. But I'm home to stay now and we'll have some really great times together when you're feeling better."

Buster smiled and closed his eyes, one arm around Chopper.

14

The band played "Advance Australia Fair." The crowd cheered. Buster was so proud, he thought he'd burst! His chest swelled. He and Chopper stood on the steps of the Town Hall. The mayor was beside them, decked in ceremonial robes. Next to him was the chief of police — the brass buttons on his jacket glistened in the sunlight.

Dad, Aunt Tilly, Ned, and Danny's parents sat in the front row of chairs that had been arranged in the Town Square for the ceremony. Behind them the whole of Coolabah Public School was spread out — principal, teachers, and students — even a subdued McGinty. Most of the people of Coolabah were there.

The mayor boomed into the microphone. "Ladies and gentlemen, boys and girls! We are gathered here today, to honor this boy and this dog."

Good grief, thought Buster. Sounds like we're getting married! He caught Erin's eye. She was sitting near the front, in her school uniform, her blond hair neatly braided. She winked and Buster stifled a giggle.

The mayor continued — a long speech about the bravery of Buster and Chopper; how they'd risked their own lives to try and help a friend, etcetera, etcetera.

Buster's mind wandered.

The rescuers hadn't asked how Danny had made it to the top of the cliff while Buster was still at the bottom. Perhaps they thought Buster had fallen down while helping Danny. Who knows! Whatever they thought, the secret was safe.

Only Ned had made a comment. "Just as well that dog is so smart," he'd said quietly.

Buster had stared at Ned. But Ned had just smiled a small, secret smile and walked off.

Buster's mind came back to the ceremony as the mayor wound up his speech.

"And so it is with great pleasure, that I ask our police chief to present bravery medals to Buster Thompson and Chopper!"

A roar of cheers and applause erupted from the crowd. The police chief stepped forward. He hung the medal around Buster's neck, shook his hand, then stopped and hung a medal around Chopper's neck. Chopper shook hands also.

The mayor invited everyone to stay for afternoon tea. It was spread out on trestle tables under the shade of trees. Buster and Chopper joined the

throng. Everyone crowded around to offer their congratulations.

"It's a pity Danny couldn't be here today," said Danny's mom.

"I'll go and see him tonight," Buster replied. "Show him my medal. And Chopper's!"

"Come and have some afternoon tea," the mayor's wife said and steered Buster away with her hand under his elbow. "There's lots to eat. Sausage rolls, pizza, sandwiches, and even some of your Aunt Tilly's famous apple pie and pudding."

Chopper's ears pricked up.

"Not now!" Buster hissed and pushed the dog's head down below the table.

Erin appeared, as Buster was munching on a sausage roll dripping with tomato sauce.

"I wish you didn't have to go back to the city," she sighed.

"I'll be back. That's a promise. To see you and Danny and all the gang. Maybe during school holidays. Besides, I have to come back and visit Chopper. I wanted to take him with me, but Ned said he's a country dog and wouldn't have enough space in the city."

"Have you been to the hospital to see Danny?" Erin asked.

"Yep. I've been several times. He's starting to get bored now that he's feeling better. Looks like his leg will be in traction for a couple of months.

We should take him some of this party food. He said he's sick of hospital meals already."

"Might see you later tonight then," said Erin as she gathered food onto a paper plate.

"Sure thing," Buster grinned.

Buster and Chopper circled outside the children's ward, waiting for the night nurse to finish her rounds. Her flashlight flickered across the sleeping patients.

When she went back into her office, the helicopter zoomed in through the window. A row of beds lined the long, enclosed veranda. Startled heads came out from under blankets, where they'd settled for the night.

Chopper's motor whirred and his red eyes flashed, as he and Buster hovered above the amazed patients. Danny was in the end bed, his mouth open and his eyes wide.

Buster, triumphant, held up a tray.

"Anyone for pizza?"

About the Author

LEIGH TRESEDER was born the second of five children in Sydney, Australia. As a child she was an avid reader and the local librarian had difficulty keeping up with Leigh's demand for books. She also loved to tell stories and dreamed of becoming a writer. Unfortunately, circumstances prevented this, so after graduating from school she studied nursing — but her desire to write never faded and Ms. Treseder's first attempt at writing for children resulted in *My Dog Can Fly!*, originally published by Ashton Scholastic as *Bustard's Custard*.

Ms. Treseder lives in Sydney, Australia, with her husband and two children.

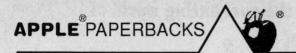

APPLE® PAPERBACKS

Pick an Apple and Polish Off Some Great Reading!

BEST-SELLING APPLE TITLES

- ❏ MT43944-8 **Afternoon of the Elves** Janet Taylor Lisle   **$2.75**
- ❏ MT43109-9 **Boys Are Yucko** Anna Grossnickle Hines   **$2.95**
- ❏ MT43473-X **The Broccoli Tapes** Jan Slepian   **$2.95**
- ❏ MT40961-1 **Chocolate Covered Ants** Stephen Manes   **$2.95**
- ❏ MT45436-6 **Cousins** Virginia Hamilton   **$2.95**
- ❏ MT44036-5 **George Washington's Socks** Elvira Woodruff   **$2.95**
- ❏ MT45244-4 **Ghost Cadet** Elaine Marie Alphin   **$2.95**
- ❏ MT44351-8 **Help! I'm a Prisoner in the Library** Eth Clifford   **$2.95**
- ❏ MT43618-X **Me and Katie (The Pest)** Ann M. Martin   **$2.95**
- ❏ MT43030-0 **Shoebag** Mary James   **$2.95**
- ❏ MT46075-7 **Sixth Grade Secrets** Louis Sachar   **$2.95**
- ❏ MT42882-9 **Sixth Grade Sleepover** Eve Bunting   **$2.95**
- ❏ MT41732-0 **Too Many Murphys** Colleen O'Shaughnessy McKenna   **$2.95**

Available wherever you buy books, or use this order form.

Scholastic Inc., P.O. Box 7502, 2931 East McCarty Street, Jefferson City, MO 65102

Please send me the books I have checked above. I am enclosing $_____ (please add $2.00 to cover shipping and handling). Send check or money order — no cash or C.O.D.s please.

Name_____ Birthdate_____

Address _____

City_____ State/Zip _____

Please allow four to six weeks for delivery. Offer good in the U.S.A. only. Sorry, mail orders are not available to residents of Canada. Prices subject to change.

APP693

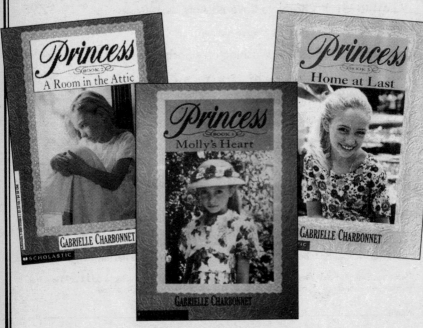